GET A CLUE

OPERATION
GOLDEN SCEPTER

A PICTURE MYSTERY

GET A CLUE

OPERATION
GOLDEN SCEPTER
A PICTURE MYSTERY

Julian Press

GROSSET & DUNLAP

GROSSET & DUNLAP

Published by the Penguin Group

Penguin Group (USA) Inc., 375 Hudson Street, New York, New York 10014, USA

Penguin Group (Canada), 90 Eglinton Avenue East, Suite 700, Toronto, Ontario M4P 2Y3, Canada

(a division of Pearson Penguin Canada Inc.)

Penguin Books Ltd., 80 Strand, London WC2R 0RL, England

Penguin Group Ireland, 25 St. Stephen's Green, Dublin 2, Ireland

(a division of Penguin Books Ltd.)

Penguin Group (Australia), 250 Camberwell Road, Camberwell, Victoria 3124, Australia

(a division of Pearson Australia Group Pty. Ltd.)

Penguin Books India Pvt. Ltd., 11 Community Centre, Panchsheel Park, New Delhi—110 017, India

Penguin Group (NZ), 67 Apollo Drive, Rosedale, North Shore 0632, New Zealand

(a division of Pearson New Zealand Ltd.)

Penguin Books (South Africa) (Pty.) Ltd., 24 Sturdee Avenue,

Rosebank, Johannesburg 2196, South Africa

Penguin Books Ltd., Registered Offices:

80 Strand, London WC2R 0RL, England

Copyright © 2006 by cbj Verlag, a division of Verlagsgrupped Random House GmbH, Munchen, Germany.
Translated and adapted by the Miller Literary Agency, LLC. All rights reserved.
Cover background copyright © Mayang Murni Adnin, 2001-2006.
Published by Grosset & Dunlap in 2008, a division of Penguin Young Readers Group,
345 Hudson Street, New York, New York 10014.
GROSSET & DUNLAP is a trademark of Penguin Group (USA) Inc.
Printed in the U.S.A.

Library of Congress Control Number: 2007049041

ISBN 978-0-448-44874-9   10 9 8 7 6 5 4 3 2 1

NTRODUCTION

The Sugar Shack sold the best candy in Hillsdale, the tiny town where best friends Josh, David, and Lily lived. The Sugar Shack was owned by Lily Shipman's uncle, Frank. Lily, David, and Josh spent a lot of time there after school. Sometimes Lily's other uncle, Tony, dropped by. Tony was a police detective and a sucker for lollipops. The three friends loved mysteries, suspense stories, and solving puzzles, so they constantly harassed Tony with questions about his work. One day Tony suggested they start up their own detective agency. They could use the candy storage room in the attic of the Sugar Shack as their headquarters, and Frank and Tony could be their technical consultants. The three friends jumped at the chance! It was no time at all before they solved their very first case . . .

MEET THE DETECTIVES

 Frank Shipman, the owner of the Sugar Shack, is like some of the chocolates he sells: tough on the outside, gooey on the inside.

 Josh Rigby has eagle eyes and loves gadgets. His pockets are always full of tools to use in unexpected situations.

 Lily Shipman is extremely athletic. She's fast and competitive. She loves a good challenge.

 Inspector Tony Shipman is a computer whiz. He gave his old computer to the detectives, who sometimes use it when working on a case.

 David Doyle has a sensitive ear, especially for birdcalls. The clucking of his loyal cockatoo, Robinson, is like a second language to him.

 Robinson the cockatoo is David's sidekick. More than one criminal has gotten into a flap with Robinson's wings.

You can help Lily, David, Josh, and friends solve the mysteries in this book. Just read the stories, and try to answer the questions. Here's a hint: Look at the pictures for clues!

CLUE ONE: I Can't See Inside!

A few days before school let out for spring break, Lily, David, and Josh met at the Ice Cream Palace after school. While David snuck pieces of his sugar cone to Robinson, Josh finished his math homework and Lily worked on a crossword puzzle.

"Six letters, the clue is 'flying thief.' The fifth letter is *i*."

"That's easy," said David. "It's magpie."

"Okay, four letters, the clue is 'be quiet.'"

"Shhh!" said Josh suddenly, looking up from his homework. "I hear people talking in the storefront next door, but it's supposed to be empty while repairs are being done."

"It's probably the construction workers," Lily suggested. After a few moments she reconsidered. "No, that can't be right. Why would they be speaking so quietly? It can't be them, so who are they?" She leaned in to listen. "And who is this Ludwig they keep mentioning?"

Lily went outside to take a look, but the door was locked and the windows were so dirty that she couldn't see anything. "It's no use. The windows are too dirty."

"We'll see about that," Josh declared as he emptied his pockets. "Look, I have just what we need to make it easier to see inside."

QUESTION: Which object will enable Josh to see through the window?

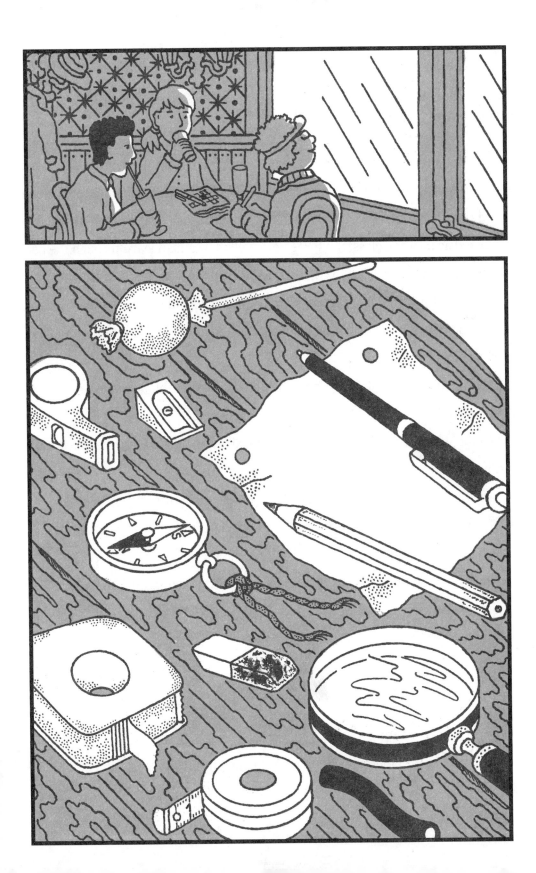

CLUE TWO: Taped

Josh took the tape and ripped off a piece, which he stuck to the window above the door. When he peeled it off, almost like magic, the glass in that spot became clean. David and Lily rushed over to peek through the hole that Josh had made. With their noses pressed against the glass, the three detectives saw a man leave through the back door. The person he was talking to couldn't be far behind.

Lily ran back into the ice cream store and quickly paid for their cones, while Josh stuffed his homework in his backpack and David jotted down a description of the man they saw through the glass.

"Black cap with a white pom-pom, turtleneck sweater, blond hair, and a prominent chin. Okay, let's go! We don't want to lose him!"

By the time the kids rushed back onto the sidewalk, the man in the black cap had disappeared.

The next day, the detectives met during recess to discuss their new case.

"Those two men seem like they're up to no good, but we need to figure out exactly what they're doing."

"You won't believe this!" David exclaimed as he looked through the fence. "Look over there. I see him!"

QUESTION: Where did David spot the man from the Ice Cream Palace?

CLUE THREE: There's the Pom-pom!

"He put his hat on the luggage rack of his motorcycle!" exclaimed Josh.

"A motorcycle which, as far as I can tell, has no license plate," David commented.

There was no time left to talk about the mystery, though. Recess ended and Josh, David, and Lily went back inside to take their last tests before spring break. Josh wrote an essay about a poem, David took a math test, and Lily made a presentation about the lives of the medieval kings of Europe. When the detectives met up again after school, they were smiling. They had aced their tests, and school was officially out for a whole week!

"How about we take a walk around town?" Josh proposed. "A motorcycle without a license plate and a man with a pom-pom on his hat shouldn't be too hard to find, right?"

"Look! I spot a clue!" Lily cried suddenly. "Why didn't I think of it sooner? So *that's* what the two men were talking about yesterday at the ice cream parlor! Boys, I think we're on to something."

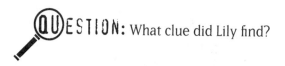 **QUESTION:** What clue did Lily find?

CLUE FOUR: A Brainstorm in the Sugar Shack

Lily saw Count Ludwig's name on a poster announcing the exhibit of his treasures at the Mansion Museum. She knew this had to be the same Ludwig the two men had mentioned several times during their secret conversation at the Ice Cream Palace.

The detectives decided to regroup back at the Sugar Shack and let Tony and Frank in on their discoveries. After discussing the clues, Frank looked up the exhibit's hours on the Internet. Tony examined David's drawing of the man with the cap and compared it to the "Most Wanted" list on the police website. No, he wasn't on the list.

"The museum has tight security. If anyone touches anything, the alarm will immediately go off. So don't waste your time looking for any clues there," said Tony.

The three detectives didn't pay any attention to Tony's warning. For three days, they stood in front of the museum, waiting for anything strange to happen. On the afternoon of the fourth day, Josh decided to give up.

"Well, Tony was right, and we were completely wrong. If the thieves were planning to steal the Count's treasure, I'm sure they would have done it by now. Let's just wait until the next group of visitors arrives, and then get out of—wait! Forget everything I just said. There he is!"

QUESTION: What did Josh notice that made him decide to stay?

CLUE FIVE: May I Offer You Some Stewe?

The man with the pom-pom hat was just emerging from an alleyway and starting to make his way toward the museum. He looked around to make sure no one was following him, then stepped up to the museum's ticket window to buy a ticket. The detectives followed him into the museum. They joined the next guided tour group. So far, everything seemed perfectly normal.

A woman with a walkie-talkie attached to her belt asked the tour group to follow her up the grand staircase and into the museum's famous Blue Room. It was there that she told the group, "The artifacts in this room are among the oldest and most precious belongings of the ancient Stewe family. This sword was forged by Count Ludwig I himself, and this golden rattle belonged to Ludwig II. Ludwig II was born in 1426 and married Elvira, of the Travers family, whose dowry included several chests full of rubies, which . . ."

The guide continued to drone away as the tour group walked from one exhibit to the next. Josh was so bored that he couldn't stop yawning as the group trailed from one display case to another. There were a lot of rooms left, too.

David stopped suddenly.

"We lost someone along the way. I'm not sure who it is yet, but someone is definitely missing."

QUESTION: Who disappeared from the tour group?

14

CLUE SIX: Freeze-Frame

"I know," said Josh, suddenly awake. "Big hat, trench coat, checkered pants. Do you think that's the—"

Before Josh could finish his question, the alarm sounded. While the rest of the tour group panicked, the three friends snuck away and retraced their steps, following the sound of the siren. In the Coronation Room, a dazed security guard gaped at pieces of broken glass in front of one of the display cases.

"This was definitely the work of a p-professional," he stammered. "He used suction cups and a diamond-edged knife!"

The three detectives left the exhibit and walked down the stairs. The head security guard was showing the director of the museum the last images before the robbery captured by the video cameras in the Coronation Room.

"As you know, sir, the security cameras take one picture of each room every thirty seconds. The thief must be here somewhere."

The pictures flashed by with no sign of the thief. Suddenly, the security guard pressed the PAUSE button. David, Lily, and Josh could just barely make out a man walking up to the display case with his hand over his face. Josh gasped. It was him!

"What are you kids doing here?" The head security guard had just noticed the detectives. "The tour is over, and now we have a mystery to solve. So please leave!"

QUESTION: What object did the robber steal?

CLUE SEVEN: A Cockatoo Makes an Excellent Watchdog

The thief stole the golden scepter that King Ronald X gave to Count Ludwig II on the morning after their victory at the Battle of Taffeton in 1451.

"But why the scepter?" Lily asked. The museum's cases were practically overflowing with jewels and precious trinkets. All of these would have been much easier to steal than the famous golden scepter. The scepter must have had a special value to the thief if he had chosen it over all of the other valuables in the museum. But what could it be? The guide led her tour group, including Josh, David, and Lily, to the exit, where the security guards searched their pockets and purses.

After going through security and exiting the museum, the detectives watched the man with the pom-pom hat walk down the steps in front of the museum, whistling to himself. David started to run after him, but Josh stopped him.

"It's not worth it," Josh said. "He's on the lookout now, and he might recognize you. Instead, let's try to find the thief. I have a feeling that he jumped out of the bathroom window to escape. Come on, let's go try to catch him!"

The three friends slid down the museum's railing and ran onto a side street. While they walked, Robinson suddenly took off from Josh's shoulder and flew into the greenery. Josh watched him.

"Shh! We have to be really quiet if we want to catch him by surprise."

 QUESTION: Who are the detectives surprising?

CLUE EIGHT: A Course through Many Courtyards

It was the thief, of course! He was hiding behind a few old oil barrels. The detectives approached him silently, but the courtyard's gravel crunched beneath their feet as they walked, which gave them away. Once he heard them coming, the thief abandoned his hiding place and climbed over the wall at the back of the courtyard with the help of a few low-hanging tree branches. The three friends heard him land with a groan on the other side of the wall. They hurried after him. This time, he wasn't going to get away!

Josh and David hopped over the fence and landed with a soft thud on the other side. "I don't believe it!" David yelled after realizing that the courtyard was empty. "He's disappeared again! Is he invisible or something?"

"It isn't going to be easy to find him in here," Josh muttered, looking around at all the overgrown trees and bushes. "Look how many hiding places there are!"

Lily was still sitting on the top of the wall. She used her vantage point to look around for any clues the detectives may have missed in the courtyard. She looked high and low, and was just about to give up when a tiny detail caught her eye.

"Hey, Josh and David! Do you see what I see?" she cried to the boys, pointing in the direction of her discovery. "Either he lost it, or he wanted to get rid of it."

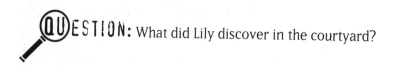 **QUESTION:** What did Lily discover in the courtyard?

CLUE NINE: Hot off the Presses

Lily jumped down from the fence and collected the thief's hat, which was sticking out from under the staircase. She decided to bring it back to the Sugar Shack to examine it more closely. As for the hat's owner, he was long gone.

The next day, Frank and Tony knocked on the door of the detectives' office in the Sugar Shack, which also doubled as the store's candy storage room. Frank and Tony showed the detectives a copy of the *Northern News*. On the front page, next to a photo of the golden scepter, was an article detailing the theft. The beginning of the article didn't offer any new information, but suddenly Frank read something that made everyone pay very close attention.

"The scepter was one of the museum's recent acquisitions," he read aloud. "It was part of an inheritance from the late Professor Alphonse Norton. The mystery surrounding the circumstances in which the famous archeologist came to own the scepter was never solved. Just after his death, his housekeeper and sole heir proposed donating the scepter—"

"Another mystery!" Lily interrupted. "Let's investigate!"

Luckily, the detectives found the professor's address in the yellow pages. His apartment was one of two rooms above a pizzeria. There were no names on the doors, so Lily rang a doorbell at random. A friendly-looking, middle-aged woman answered the door. David leaned toward Josh.

"Yes, that's definitely the housekeeper. And this is definitely Norton's apartment."

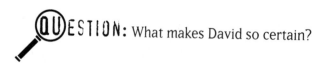 **QUESTION:** What makes David so certain?

CLUE TEN: Tears for the Teacher

The three detectives introduced themselves, and explained why they were there. After they were finished, the housekeeper burst into tears.

"It's so nice of you to try to clear up this horrible mess! The poor professor was so attached to his scepter. Fortunately, the painting of him holding it is still hanging right here! Do come in, I was just about to order something to eat. How about a pizza?"

The housekeeper's offer was too good to resist. Josh, David, and Lily happily gulped down slices of pepperoni and extra-cheese pizza while the housekeeper told them the story of her life. When the three friends were finished eating, they thanked her and left.

"Living above a pizza shop would be great, but it can't be fun to live all alone," Josh said to his friends.

David and Lily sadly nodded their heads in agreement as they walked down the stairs and back out into the street. Compared to the peace and quiet of the professor's apartment, the street noise was loud. The detectives realized that even though they'd spent an entire afternoon with the housekeeper, they hadn't made any progress on their case. How did Norton get the scepter in the first place?

A car horn suddenly sounded, making Josh jump. He couldn't believe his eyes. These criminals definitely weren't afraid of wearing loud clothing!

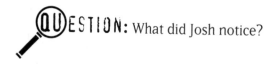 **QUESTION:** What did Josh notice?

CLUE ELEVEN: Checkered Chase

"Personally, if I were a thief on the run from the police, I would at least change my pants," Josh joked. "And not wear those ridiculous checkered things. The light's green, let's go follow him!"

The detectives ran after the thief with the checkered pants. The man jumped on a bicycle and started to pedal furiously. The detectives ran as fast as they could to try to catch him. With Lily at the head of the pack, the three friends closed the gap between them and the bicycling thief little by little. Eventually, they found themselves only a few feet behind the robber, when he turned sharply and disappeared behind an iron gate. The detectives ran up to the gate, but it slammed shut before they could get through. On the other side of the gate, there was a large house with thick trees and bushes surrounding it.

David boosted Lily up to get a better look. She examined the garden and house, looking for clues.

"Other than a car in one corner, the property seems deserted," she reported as she jumped down.

"So the thief must have had a control to open the iron gate?" Josh asked.

"It seems like it," Lily pondered. "Hey, look, Robinson is exploring the garden. He's excited about something!"

She climbed back onto David's shoulders.

"Someone was just here, I'm sure of it!" Lily cried out.

 **QUESTION:** What did Lily notice?

CLUE TWELVE: By Gnome!

The garden gnome on the left side of the lawn wasn't looking in the same direction as it was the first time Lily saw it. Lily jumped off of David's shoulders, landed on top of the gate, and jumped down into the grass on the other side of the fence. She tiptoed quietly through the garden's bushes toward the gnome. His beard looked like it was detachable, so she gave it a tug. The gnome was positioned on some kind of rotating device, and spun 180 degrees! As the gnome turned around in a circle, Lily heard a groaning, scraping noise from the other side of the garden.

Lily rushed over to where the noise was coming from. It was a worn and rusty drain cover that had opened, revealing a flight of stairs. Lily rushed down the stairs, using the tiny stream of light that trickled through the tunnel's entrance as her guide. At the end of the underground tunnel, she opened a door that was already slightly ajar and found herself inside the large house. She quietly walked up another flight of stairs to the ground floor. The first door she tried was the right one!

In the dark, incredibly messy office she found the stolen scepter, which had been left on a chair. The scepter lay in two pieces, and Lily suddenly understood why. The robber wasn't interested in the scepter; he was interested in whatever was hidden *inside* the scepter! What was the scepter's secret?

Her heart pounding, Lily looked around the room. Suddenly, she froze.

"That's the key to the mystery!" she whispered to herself.

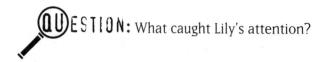 **QUESTION:** What caught Lily's attention?

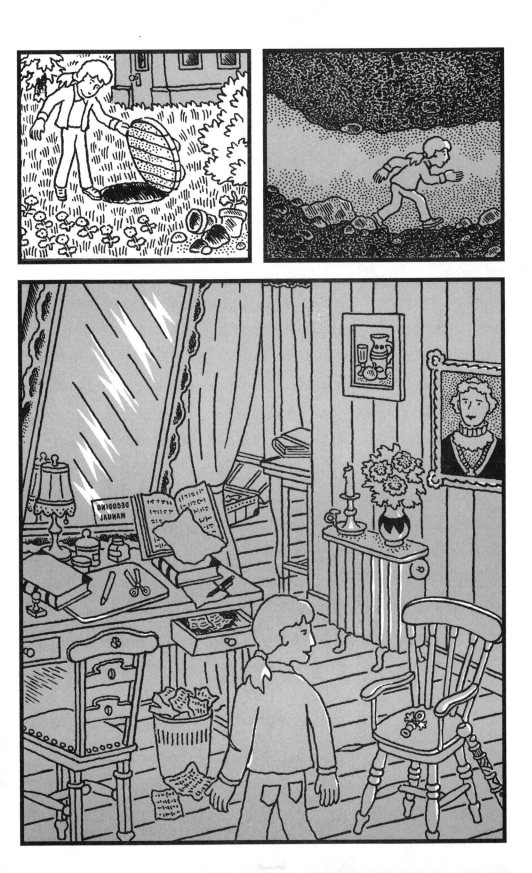

CLUE THIRTEEN: Shivers and Shuffles

The glass reflected the title of the book that lay open on the desk: *Decoding Manual.* Underneath the book, Lily spotted a crumpled piece of paper: the contents of the scepter! Lily grabbed the paper and opened it. The paper was yellowed and ancient-looking, and on it she spotted a series of strange symbols that were all jumbled together. A secret message, no doubt!

Careful not to disturb anything, Lily searched through the wastepaper basket for any clues. It was filled with crumpled-up pieces of paper that looked a lot like the one she was holding in her hand. The thief must have started to decode the secret message.

A loud noise made Lily jump. Even though she felt afraid, she tried to convince herself that it must have been the wind in the trees or just the creaking of the old house.

Now, what to do about decoding the message? She couldn't carry the decoding book back through the tunnel; it was too big and heavy.

She grabbed the original secret message and a rough draft of the key to the code, which had a mysterious alphabet written on it. She had to run, and not back through the tunnel—its entrance was too far away. It would be easier to escape through a nearby window. Just as she was about to make a run for it, she heard a noise. What if the thief was there with her in the room, watching her every move? She turned around and gasped at what she saw in front of her. There seemed to be someone else in the room!

QUESTION: What made Lily suspect there was someone else in the room?

CLUE FOURTEEN: Curtains for Lily

The curtain hanging in front of the window was short enough to reveal the tips of a pair of men's shoes sticking out. At a glance, Lily calculated the distance that separated her from the hallway and from the glass door on the veranda. With any luck, she would be able to escape. But how would she get over the garden wall? She decided to figure that out later, and take it one step at a time. Suddenly, the wind blew through the open door and caused the curtain to billow out. Lily almost fainted with relief: She was planning her escape from an empty pair of shoes!

After a few moments of shock, Lily pulled herself together. *The man must be somewhere in the house*, she thought to herself. She strained to hear him, but she could only hear her own heart pounding. She tiptoed across the hallway. Her fingers shook as she grabbed the knob of the veranda door, which opened with a groan. Lily quickly ran out of the house.

The ladder that she'd spotted earlier was still there. She carried it over to the gate, leaned it carefully against the wall, and quickly climbed up it. As she jumped down to the other side of the gate, David and Josh ran over to hug her. They were so relieved she was safe!

The detectives regrouped back at the Sugar Shack. Lily told them the story of her adventure inside the creepy house. The detectives studied the alphabet and secret message that Lily had found until finally they were able to decode it! Frank copied the message out for them.

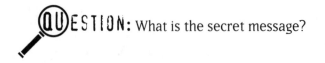 QUESTION: What is the secret message?

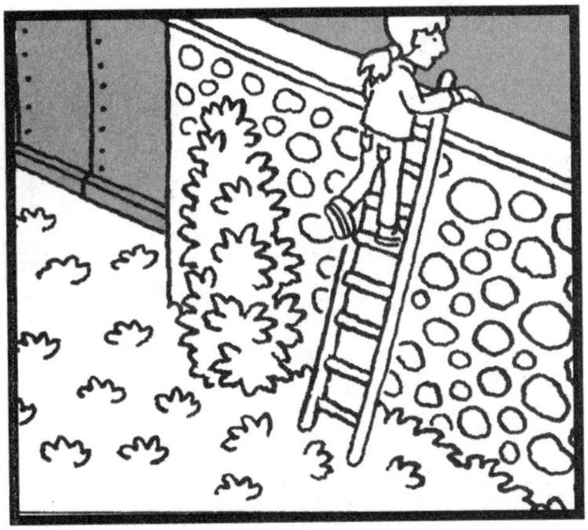

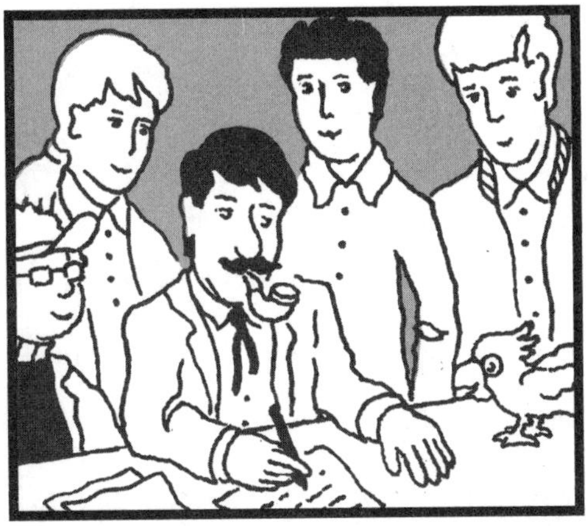

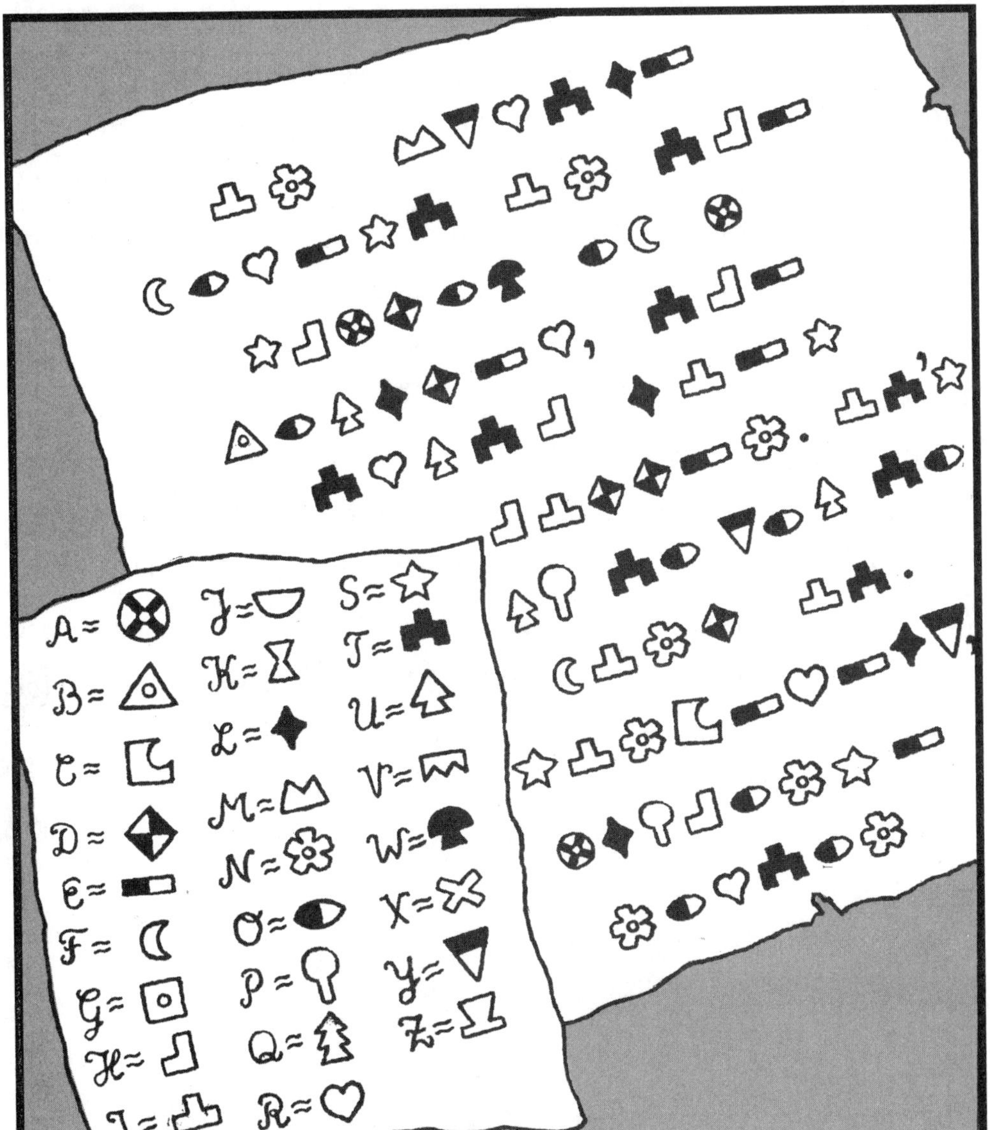
A =
B =
C =
D =
E =
F =
G =
H =
I =
J =
K =
L =
M =
N =
O =
P =
Q =
R =
S =
T =
U =
V =
W =
X =
Y =
Z =

CLUE FIFTEEN: The Message

The message confused them even more. Frank read it aloud: "In Myrtle Forest in the shadow of a boulder, the truth lies hidden. It's up to you to find it. Sincerely, Alphonse Norton."

Tony paced back and forth, careful to avoid the low-hanging ceiling beams in the gang's headquarters. "Let's keep at it," he encouraged them. "Here is the evidence we have so far: Professor Norton hid a message in the scepter, which he willed to his housekeeper after he died. She sold it to the museum, and then it was stolen shortly thereafter. Which leads us to our first question: Where did Norton find the scepter in the first place? And that question leads us to a *second* question: What is the 'hidden truth' that the robber was so interested in? I've made a decision. Everyone, get into the car! Let's investigate Myrtle Forest. But kids, you have to stay together when we go in. It could be dangerous."

After a quick drive, the detectives, Frank, and Tony found themselves at the edge of Myrtle Forest. Even though it was spooky, they bravely entered the forest, hoping to find some clues. After walking for about an hour, the group reached a clearing that had a boulder in the middle. They examined the boulder from all angles and inspected every crevice, even its smallest hole. Perched on a fir tree, Robinson amused himself by imitating a blue jay. Suddenly, he whistled sharply.

"I found it!" cried Josh, who followed the bird's gaze.

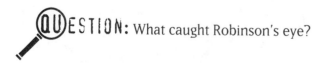 **QUESTION:** What caught Robinson's eye?

CLUE SIXTEEN: A Rock Garden

As the afternoon sun broke through the clouds, Josh noticed something on the side of the boulder gleaming in the light. It was an iron ring! Josh took out his magnifyir glass from his backpack. One part of the ring shone like it had been recently polished, but the other side was covered in rust. Plus, there were tiny particles of rust on the rock where the ring was attached to it. Frank congratulated Josh for finding the ring with an approving wink.

"Open sesame!" Josh exclaimed, pulling vigorously on the ring. The rock wall slowly slid over, revealing a large staircase cut into it.

"So there's more here than meets the eye," he murmured to himself. "Come on, guys, let's go explore!"

They quietly tiptoed down the stairs in a single-file line. Robinson led the way; he seemed to know exactly where he was going. Ahead of them, the narrow passageway opened up into a giant cave filled with glistening stalagmites. Fat drops of water fell from the ceiling. A group of bats fled from the dark cave, frightened by the beam of light coming from Frank's flashlight.

"Stop!" Tony cried suddenly. "Someone has been here. I have proof!"

QUESTION: What proves that someone had recently been prowling around in the cave?

CLUE SEVENTEEN: Achoo!

Tony's proof was right there in the middle of a pile of stones. He picked up the abandoned flashlight carefully with a piece of paper from his pocket: He didn't want to damage the fingerprints on it.

"It feels warm, which means that whoever was using it must—"

Tony stopped talking suddenly. A scary hooting noise echoed through the cave.

"It's the ghost of Count Ludwig, coming back to reclaim his scepter!" Josh joked as a shiver ran down his spine.

"Not quite, Josh," David declared. "It's the call of the cave owl, which nests in caverns like this. It's a rare bird whose babies . . ."

"Achoo!" Frank's sneeze interrupted David's explanation. "Excuse me, but this musty old cave is aggravating my allergies. Plus, I'm soaking wet. Aren't you guys? Achoo!"

"Shh!" said Josh. "Listen. I hear groaning."

"Then it must be Ludwig's ghost," said Lily, teasing Josh. "He stubbed his toe on a rock because he doesn't have a flashlight."

"No," said Tony. "Josh is right. Somebody *human* is in trouble. Look!"

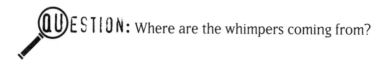 **QUESTION:** Where are the whimpers coming from?

CLUE EIGHTEEN: An Unforeseen Encounter

Tony spotted two hands clinging to the side of a crevice in the rock. The detectives could just make out the red and sweaty face of the person whose hands were holding on tightly, about to slip. The man looked like he was about to lose his grip and fall into the chasm below. He gasped in pain, and screamed out to them, "Take pity on me! Help! Don't let me fall!"

Tony and Frank quickly helped the man up. The three detectives recognized his checkered pants right away. Tony handcuffed him; he had seen this man before.

"Bernard Livingston! What a lovely surprise! Did you get bored outside of prison?" Tony asked the thief sarcastically.

"You've got it all wrong, officer," Livingston protested meekly. "It's Paul the Pom-pom and his girlfriend who organized everything. I just *pretended* to be in their gang so I could . . . um . . . *help you*!"

"That's a lie, Livingston. I can see right through you!" Tony told the thief. "How did you get into this cave, anyway?"

"I . . . um . . . I'm interested in caves, sir."

"Oh, okay. I'll make sure they give you an underground cell, then."

"You have no proof against me!" Livingston cried.

"We'll see about that," Tony replied.

"I'd even say that we've *seen* about that," Frank added. "Kids, do you see what I'm talking about?"

QUESTION: What proof against Livingston did Frank discover?

CLUE NINETEEN: Victim's Vengeance

David shimmied up the stalagmite and grabbed the mysterious package. Tony opened it, and much to everyone's surprise, took out a second identical golden scepter. At the police station, Bernard Livingston finally confessed everything.

"It's a very complicated story," he told the police officers. "Alphonse Norton was a distant cousin of Duke Terrell and a descendant of Count Ludwig. Twenty years ago, the professor, who was jealous that his cousin owned the scepter, paid Paul the Pom-pom a large sum of money to steal it. Paul stole the scepter and replaced it with a fake that Norton had made. Then, instead of paying him, Norton threatened to blackmail him and tell the police. After Duke Terrell died, his cousin inherited the scepter, but only Norton and Paul knew it was a fake. The real scepter has a sapphire as big as an egg . . ."

"Which must be worth a lot of money," interrupted the officer in charge of the interrogation.

"Yes, a fortune that Paul hoped to take back after the professor's death."

"And he chose you as his accomplice?"

"Yes . . . well, no. I mean . . . well, anyway, I was planning to turn him in to the police when I had enough evidence," Livingston said, trying to make himself seem less guilty.

QUESTION: What small detail distinguished the real scepter from the copy?

CLUE ONE: Bad News Bird

The sapphire on the real scepter was placed vertically, while the fake stone was accidentally placed horizontally. Paul the Pom-pom and his gang of thieves (which even included the museum tour guide!) were arrested the same day and joined Bernard Livingston in police custody, awaiting their trial. The director of the museum blamed what happened on himself, saying that he should have noticed the scepter was a fake, and resigned. The local newspaper ran a long article about the case of Ludwig's scepter. It featured a story about Lily, Josh, and David and their detective work. The mayor offered the detectives tickets to see *The Thieving Magpie* at the theater downtown as a reward for their hard work.

On the night of the premiere, David, Lily, and Josh dressed up and took their seats in a box in the first tier. The theater was packed. The lights began to go down, and the first notes of the overture sounded through the theater. The last sounds of whispered conversations floated through the theater air and abruptly ended as everyone's eyes turned toward the lush red velvet curtains that were slowly opening. Suddenly, a cry rang out. Murmurs of alarm sounded across the audience, and the overhead lights came back on. The three detectives searched the audience to see where the cry had come from.

"It's the woman in blue," said David. "I think she fainted."

 **QUESTION:** Where is the woman in blue?

CLUE TWO: Nothing to Fear but Fear Itself

"Follow me!" David whispered to his friends as he jumped up from his seat and took off into the hallway.

Josh, David, and Lily made it over to the third balcony just as the woman in blue was recovering from her fainting spell. An usher handed her a glass of water. The woman swallowed one tiny sip, and then, with her hand on her bare throat, gave a strangled, tearful cry.

"My necklace! It was all that remained of my grandmother!"

In a trembling voice, she told the people around her about how she had felt a hand close around her throat and unhook her beloved necklace while the theater was dark.

While the theater director explained to the police what had happened and the ushers asked the audience to take their seats, the detectives rushed out of the theater to track down the thief.

A few feet from the theater's entrance, they found an old lady clinging to a fence shaking with fear. She told them that a man had raced out of the theater, bumped into her and nearly knocked her over.

He didn't steal anything, she told them. Could she describe him? No, she couldn't, it had all happened so fast. Josh, David, and Lily asked if she would like them to walk her home.

"Oh, thank you, children, but it's all right. It's very nice of you to offer."

The kids turned the corner and Lily saw something that made her realize the thief had just been there.

QUESTION: How did she know the thief had passed that way?

CLUE THREE: A Suspicious Roar

Looking through the bushes, Lily found a glove. It looked like a brand-new motorcycle glove.

"The thief must not be too bright to have dropped evidence," Josh said.

"Or he might be so confident that he thinks he can afford to be sloppy," David reflected.

"Which could be our opportunity," Lily chimed in. "Because when a thief is feeling too sure of himself, he's bound to make mistakes."

Hiding in the shadows of houses and walking in single file, the detectives crept along the street without a sound. Suddenly, Robinson lifted his head and flapped his wings wildly, his secret sign to alert the gang to danger. The next moment, the roar of a motorcycle interrupted the silence that hung over the street. The noise grew louder as the motorcycle drew closer. At that exact moment, a cloud crossed over the moon, plunging the square into almost complete darkness.

Soon, headlights washed over the facades of the buildings, and the darkness returned as the noise faded away. The lantern outside the Traveler's Hotel provided a tiny glow of light.

"We'll never catch him now," David decided. "Let's go back to the theater!"

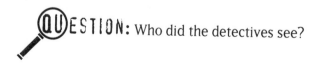

QUESTION: Who did the detectives see?

CLUE FOUR: Again!

Just as he passed under the light outside the Traveler's Hotel, the three friends saw the man on the motorcycle. On their walk back to the theater, the detectives discussed whether they were on the right track at all to finding the thief.

"Just because we found a motorcycle glove doesn't mean we should suspect the first person we see on a motorcycle," Josh said.

The intermission was just starting when the detectives arrived back at the theater. The crowd was noisy, but not one word was being spoken about the show. Instead, everyone was buzzing about the theft of the necklace. The detectives decided to use this opportunity to hunt for clues. Listening carefully, the detectives moved from one group of people to another, picking up bits of each conversation.

"Scandalous!"

"Unheard of!"

"What times we live in, my friends. What's next, I ask you?"

Lily was surprised that nobody was talking about how sad the woman must be to have lost the only reminder she had of her grandmother. The theater chimes rang, announcing the beginning of the second act. Nearby, a woman fell into a chair, weeping.

"The thief strikes again," David whispered in Lily's ear.

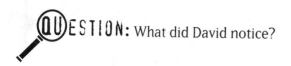 **QUESTION:** What did David notice?

CLUE FIVE: Lily's Rampage

Distracted by their conversations, the audience members didn't notice anything, and took their seats. The theater director quietly ordered all the doors locked. The thief had struck again, stealing a bracelet from the woman David saw crying.

"I was leaving the bathroom when I realized it was gone," she hiccuped.

"We'll find it, ma'am, we promise!" Josh said as Lily and David dragged him away.

"Why did you guys pull me away?" he asked.

"Shhh! Be quiet and follow us," Lily told him. "David just saw a man run through that door at the end of the lobby."

"It was probably an employee who had to check on something," he told them. "We shouldn't jump to conclusions and assume he's doing something wrong."

"Are you too afraid to check it out? You know that we can't be sure until we investigate," David said.

Josh followed David and Lily through the door, even though he was annoyed. The door led to the basement. The detectives groped along in the darkness, holding on to the wall as a guide. They heard footsteps along the corridor, and then a loud *CRASH!* David, Josh, and Lily took off in the direction of the loud noise. When the detectives finally stopped running, they found themselves in a huge room filled with props and scenery.

"It's too late!" Lily fumed. "He's gone."

QUESTION: Why was Lily sure the thief had already left the scene of the crime?

CLUE SIX: Twins

The wind knocked the shutters of the window through which the thief had escape
The detectives could just barely hear the sound of a motorcycle speeding away. Finally,
Josh admitted that they had been on the right track all along and apologized to his frier

The detectives decided that after escaping with the necklace, the thief had
returned to the scene of the crime. He'd snuck in through the basement window, mingle
with the crowd during intermission, and successfully stolen a diamond bracelet withou
its owner noticing. What nerve!

The next night, Frank and Tony went to the production of *The Thieving Magpie*.
Frank observed the entire theater through his binoculars from his position on the
balcony, while Tony encouraged him to put the binoculars away and enjoy the show.

"Stop staring at everyone, Frank! People are starting to look at you. Do you
honestly think that the thief would come back after last night? Take it from a police
inspector: He won't!"

Frank put his binoculars away, but took them out again during the second act.
After a few moments, his jaw dropped in shock. He silently handed the binoculars to
his brother.

"My word!" said Tony, the binoculars still pressed against his eyes. "I don't
believe it!"

"Never say never," Frank said with a grim smile. "Take it from a candy store
owner!"

QUESTION: What did Tony and Frank spot through the binoculars?

CLUE SEVEN: Encore

In a box on the second tier, a hand reached out from behind the curtain to steal another diamond necklace! Tony and Frank leaped from their seats, apologizing to the people seated around them. The usher at the door refused to let them leave before the show was over, until Tony showed her his police badge. That did the trick. The two brothers strategically positioned themselves at the top of the grand staircase. From this height, they were able to observe the flood of audience members that tumbled out of the theater and toward the bar after the act was over.

"What masterful work! So cool and collected!" Frank commented. "That poor woman has no idea her necklace is missing . . . yet."

"No, this could be good!" Tony chimed in. "If we catch the thief before the woman notices her necklace is gone, we could prevent another scandal."

"I agree, but in order to catch him, we'll have to find him in this crowd," Frank sighed.

"Do you remember anything specific about the thief? Anything unique? He made a big mistake wearing those gloves."

"That may be, but if he's smart, he'll keep his hands in his pockets."

"Then he's not as smart as you think he is. That's him, there!"

 **QUESTION:** How did Tony recognize the thief?

CLUE EIGHT: With Your Heart in Your Mouth and the Cops on Your Heels

The man standing by the mirror, pretending to read the program, was no innocent audience member! Tony and Frank recognized him by the reflection of a heart stitched into his left glove. It was identical to the glove on the hand they'd seen stealing the diamond necklace!

"Let's go, but quietly and discreetly," Tony whispered. Pretending to be deeply involved in a conversation about the show, the two brothers slowly approached the bar. They occasionally turned to look at the man, who didn't move.

"What can I get you gentlemen?" the bartender asked Frank and Tony.

As soon as he saw Frank and Tony were distracted, the thief sprinted away. He wriggled between the people crowding the lobby and disappeared behind a door. Tony and Frank took off after him. He was headed to the door at the far end of the lobby! The kids had told them about this door. Frank and Tony shuffled down the stairs and ran down the long, dark corridor to the prop room. What the thief and the two brothers didn't know was that during the performance, the theater director had ordered the window to be boarded up. The thief was trapped.

"Do you see him?" Frank whispered to Tony.

"He got rid of the necklace before he hid," Tony said with a nod.

 QUESTION: Where did the robber leave his loot? And where is he hiding?

CLUE NINE: David on the Lookout

"If you would be so kind as to come out of that trunk, sir," Tony ordered the thief while Frank, tottering on a chair, retrieved the necklace from its hiding place in the chandelier.

They handcuffed the thief and brought him to the police station, where he was identified and fingerprinted. He claimed he was innocent and had nothing to do with the thefts. The police were forced to release him on bail until they gathered more evidence.

The next morning, Frank, Josh, Lily, and David accompanied Tony, armed with a search warrant, to the suspect's apartment building. They rang his doorbell, but there was no answer. However, the door to the second-floor apartment was open. The detectives let themselves in. The smell of coffee greeted them, and Josh noticed a full cup waiting on the table. Maybe the man went downstairs to the grocery store to buy bread? It seemed like he wasn't coming back upstairs any time soon. The inspector searched the entire apartment, and then the detectives helped him put everything back in its place once he was finished. Unfortunately, there was no sign of either of the missing pieces of jewelry.

"Let's hope that the lab finds his fingerprints on the necklace, or else we won't able to convict him," Tony sighed.

"Don't give up just yet. We haven't looked *everywhere*," David declared to everyone's surprise.

QUESTION: Where did the inspector forget to look?

CLUE TEN: A Hidden Door

The door was so obvious that no one saw it, except for David. A big bureau had been placed in front of the white door. After Frank and Tony moved the bureau, they pried open the door and discovered a flight of stairs that led down to a room filled with all sorts of things.

"What a collection of junk!" Frank exclaimed. "He should open an antique store. And there's so much dust! Achoo!" Frank sneezed and blew his nose into his handkerchief. "I'll look on the left-hand side; you look in that corner, kids. Watch out for the mouse droppings! It's not very pleasant down here, is it?"

From the top of the staircase, Tony watched the group search the room while he kept an eye on the front door of the apartment.

"Oh, ew! Cockroaches! They're everywhere!" Lily screamed. She had just opened a bag filled with something smelly and rotting.

"Did you see this?" Josh exclaimed. "Raspberry jam from June, 1980. Do you think it's still good? Should I try it?" he joked.

"Stop being gross, Josh. How about helping us move this chest instead?" David suggested.

"Not so fast, David! I found it! I found the necklace and the bracelet! I am the champion!" Josh chanted loudly. "And I'm not going to tell you where it is!"

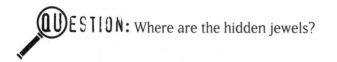

QUESTION: Where are the hidden jewels?

CLUE ONE: The House Across the Street

Lily, Josh, and David sat around a table in the Sugar Shack, reading about their latest success in the town newspaper. There was an entire article inside dedicated to Lily, Josh, and David's mystery-solving skills. There was even a photograph of the aquarium on the shelf where they'd found the stolen jewels.

"And that's that!" Josh said, putting down the paper.

"Should we get an ice cream to celebrate?" David asked.

"Definitely!" Josh answered, slipping on his jacket.

Lily didn't answer. She was seated by the window and had been strangely quiet while the boys read the newspaper.

"This is weird," she finally said. "The house across the street, number 20, seems completely abandoned."

Josh and David looked out the window. "Number 20?" Josh asked. "It's been a while since I've seen anyone inside . . ."

"Wait a second, guys. We just caught a jewel smuggler and you're already in the middle of another mystery! Can't we just go get ice cream?"

David finally convinced his friends to forget solving mysteries for a while and walk down to the Ice Cream Palace. Two hours later, on their way back to the Sugar Shack, the detectives had completely forgotten about the mystery of the house across the street. David eventually brought it up again.

"Hey, look!" he exclaimed. "It looks like someone was in the house while we were gone."

QUESTION: What evidence did the visitor leave behind?

CLUE TWO: Like Lightning

While the detectives were getting ice cream, someone had broken a basement window and gotten into the house.

"Do you think it's a robbery?" Josh asked.

"It certainly looks like it," David replied.

"Should we go take a closer look?" Lily proposed.

She didn't need to ask David and Josh twice; they were already slipping on their jackets! Two minutes later, the detectives were on the other side of the street.

"Hmm," Lily said, examining the broken glass. "There isn't any—" She interrupted herself abruptly. She'd heard someone inside the house cry for help!

Without even thinking about the danger of the situation, Lily busted down the basement window and the three detectives sprinted inside the house. They found an old lady shaking with fear in the doorway of a very messy room.

Not wanting to frighten her even more, the detectives introduced themselves. Margaret Vale explained that she was a friend of Rachel Jones, who had left her in charge of the house in her absence. Mrs. Vale started to look around to see what the robber had taken. "He didn't take any trinkets, or paintings," she began.

"Maybe he was looking for something in particular," Lily suggested.

"Sure, but what?" asked David.

"I don't know," Josh said. "But in any case, I can assure you that he found what he was looking for. Mrs. Jones's secret hiding place was no match for him."

 **QUESTION:** What hiding place is Josh talking about?

CLUE THREE: Bandit

Josh spotted a safe hanging open behind one of the paintings on the wall.

"Do you have any idea what might have been inside?" David asked Mrs. Vale.

"Not the slightest. I didn't even know Rachel had a safe," she sighed. "Don't touch anything. I'm going to call her and tell her what happened, and then call the police."

She left the room and picked up the telephone.

"What a mess," Josh whispered to the others. "Maybe we should help her clean up."

"Yeah, but for right now, I think we should leave everything as it is until the police come," Lily advised.

Suddenly, Robinson started to squawk and tried to hide his head under David's sweater.

"I'm not sure what's happened here, but Robinson is acting really weird. I think he's scared of something."

"Bandit! Bandit!"

Mrs. Vale's voice rang out from the hallway. The detectives ran over to her, thinking that the robber had returned, but found her all alone.

"Have you seen Bandit?"

They looked at her, baffled.

"He's Rachel's dog," she explained. "I hope that nothing's happened to him. Bandit, where are you? Bandit, come here . . ."

"I think Robinson found him," David announced.

QUESTION: Where is Bandit hiding?

CLUE FOUR: A Mute Witness

Robinson flew over and carefully perched on the knocked-over armchair by the window. Bandit was hiding behind it. Mrs. Vale walked slowly up to him and petted him gently on the head. "Bandit, it's me. Don't be afraid."

The little dog eventually came out of his hiding place. He had a piece of plaid fabric in his mouth. Bandit dropped the fabric on the floor and Josh picked it up.

"What is that?" Lily asked. "Do you think it belonged to the robber?"

"I don't know," said David. "But it's all the evidence we have for now."

Once the police arrived, the detectives handed over the scrap of fabric to the police to save for evidence. The police officer told the detectives that the safe contained a bar of solid gold.

"A gold bar!" Josh was still in awe after the detectives left the scene of the crime to talk the case over at the Sugar Shack.

"There's very little chance of Mrs. Jones getting it back," David remarked. "A scrap of fabric isn't very good proof of a crime."

"It is if you look around," said Lily, smiling.

David and Josh followed her gaze. They quickly realized what Lily had meant.

"The thief!" Josh exclaimed. "He hasn't even realized that his jacket is torn!"

 **QUESTION:** Where is the robber?

CLUE FIVE: A Happy Coincidence

The robber and his ripped jacket were only a few feet away. He was carrying a bi
box on one shoulder that bore an image of a black horse. The detectives started running
after him, which wasn't easy, because the street was crowded with people. They lost
precious seconds at a crosswalk, and lost sight of the thief.

"That's so frustrating," Josh said wearily. "We almost had him!"

"I think even Robinson lost sight of him," David sighed.

Lily tried to comfort them. "In any case, it's getting late. We should probably
head home anyway."

Disappointed that they had missed such a golden opportunity to solve another
mystery, the three friends walked home, dragging their feet. They soon arrived at
Halfmoon Road, near the docks.

"Do you guys want to see *Attack of the Mutant Fire Ants* tomorrow?" David
proposed, trying to change the subject.

"Maybe," Josh muttered.

"Definitely not," said Lily. "We have much more important things to do tomorrow.
I just found the black horse's trail."

QUESTION: What black horse is Lily talking about?

CLUE SIX: In the Wild West

Lily showed her friends the poster advertising the same black horse that was printed on the box that they had seen the thief carrying earlier. It was an advertisement for an outdoor show called *Old West*, which was being performed in the old quarry outside of town for the next six weeks. The friends, happy that they had found the robber's trail, split up and planned to meet the next morning.

After a good night's sleep and a long bus ride, they started investigating the quarry. The show wasn't open to the public yet, but they could still visit the quarries to see the actors rehearsing. Horses, stagecoaches, and cowboys filled the quarry. It really looked like the Wild West.

"How are we going to find the robber in there?" David asked. "We've never even seen his face!"

"Plus, he could be wearing a disguise," Lily added.

"We're not even sure he's out there!" said David.

"Yes we are," Josh said. "I can even tell you what his costume is."

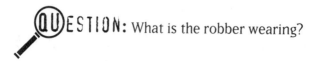 **QUESTION:** What is the robber wearing?

CLUE SEVEN: The Liar

"It must be opposite day!" Lily exclaimed. "The thief is wearing a sheriff's badge!"

"Lucky for us he's still carrying his plaid jacket," David observed.

The detectives blended into the crowd of actors and followed the fake sheriff to his caravan.

"What are you doing here?" the thief asked the detectives angrily, once he noticed they were following him. "Get out of here before I call the police!"

"You've got some nerve," Lily retorted. "It would be more appropriate for *us* to call the police, don't you think?"

"Exactly what are you insinuating?" asked the robber, unpleasantly surprised.

"You know what I'm talking about!" Lily shot back at him. She wasn't about to back down from a challenge.

"No, I don't," he said curtly.

Josh piped up. "Oh really? Mrs. Jones. The gold bar. Ring a bell?"

"Not at all!" the thief protested. "I suggest you kids get out of here and stop making accusations before I get really mad!"

"You're lying," said David calmly. "I'm sure of it. But don't worry—we're patient. We'll wait for our opportunity!"

QUESTION: How does David know that the fake sheriff is lying?

CLUE EIGHT: Bric-a-Brac

David spotted the newspaper sticking out of the pocket of the jacket hanging on the coat rack.

"The stolen gold bar is front page news today," David said, gesturing toward the newspaper.

"What? I don't know what you are talking about," the thief said, his face turning bright red. "And even if I did, what would that prove, anyway? Don't I have the right to read a newspaper?"

He rose from his armchair and pointed a finger at them menacingly.

"Get out of here before I—" The thief's threat was interrupted by him abruptly slamming the door in the detectives' faces. Josh, David, and Lily pretended to leave, and then they snuck back up to the window. The robber sat back down in his armchair and turned his back to the window. The detectives scrutinized the interior of his wagon, looking for clues.

"Do you think the gold bar is here?" Josh asked.

"Maybe," Lily replied. "Do you see the big bag over there? Maybe the thief stashed it in there."

"Or maybe he hid the gold bar in the little bag on his dresser," Josh pointed out.

"Unfortunately, we can't inspect the bags right now. But at least we know our thief's name."

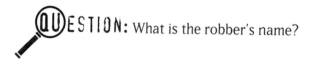

QUESTION: What is the robber's name?

CLUE NINE: The Landlady

On the table in the wagon lay an envelope addressed to Mr. Thomas Platte. Josh carefully noted the address in his notebook, and everyone agreed that they should take advantage of Mr. Platte's absence to visit his house.

An hour later, they rang the bell at his apartment. To their surprise, a well-dressed, elderly woman opened the door.

"Hello, ma'am. We're here to see Mr. Platte, please," said David politely.

"I'm sorry, he's not here right now."

"When do you expect him back?" Lily asked.

"I don't know," the woman replied. "It's been at least three weeks since he's been here."

"Tell me," she said, looking at Robinson, who was perched on David's shoulder, "are you the famous detectives? I'm sure I've seen you in the newspaper."

They blushed.

"My tenant has done nothing wrong, I hope?" she asked.

"We're not sure yet, but perhaps you could show us his room . . . ?" David asked hesitantly.

"Unfortunately," the landlady replied, "he keeps the key."

While she apologized for being unable to help them, Lily took a look through the keyhole of the room in question. Right away, she knew that Platte had been there recently.

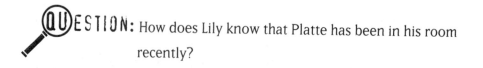 QUESTION: How does Lily know that Platte has been in his room recently?

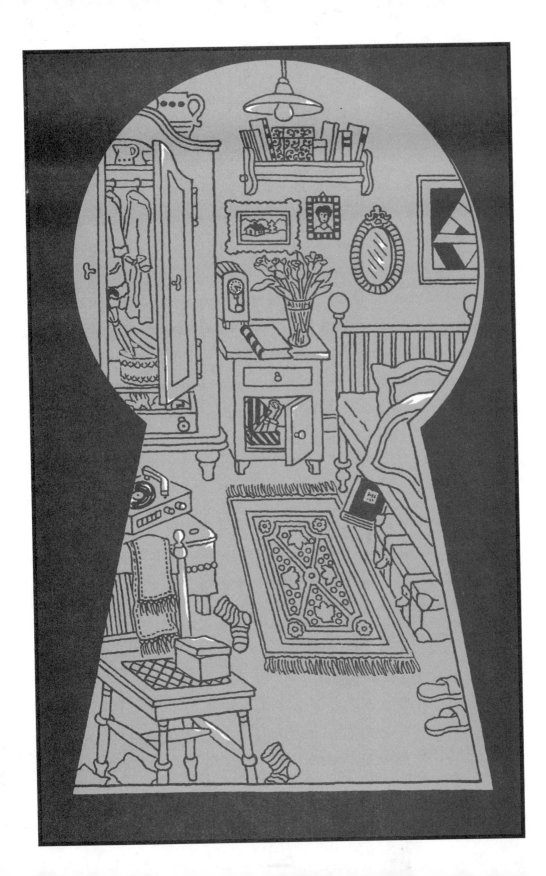

CLUE TEN: Panning for Gold

On the nightstand stood a beautiful, vibrant bouquet of roses. Flowers that had been sitting in water for three weeks would have wilted a long time ago. Therefore, Platte had been home more recently than the landlady knew—or was admitting.

The detectives decided to alert Tony and Frank as quickly as possible. Tony and Frank went to the police station to request a search warrant for Platte's apartment and wagon. Meanwhile, Josh, David, and Lily returned to the quarry to keep an eye on the thief. Unfortunately, when they arrived, they discovered that the wagon was locked and Platte had gone out. The detectives decided to mingle with the crowd of actors and look for Platte there. They eventually found him resting by the bank. Josh, David, and Lily hid behind a nearby carriage so Platte couldn't see them.

"Oh, no," Lily whispered after a few moments had passed. "I think he looked right at us!"

"Get down!" Josh ordered.

"Do you think he saw us?" Lily asked, a look of panic on her face.

"No, Lily. It's not us he's looking for," David explained. "It's the gold bar."

"The gold bar!" Josh exclaimed. "Can you see it?"

"Shh! Here he comes!"

QUESTION: How did David find the gold bar?

CLUE ELEVEN: Robinson to the Rescue

Once Platte passed the carriage without noticing the detectives hidden behind it
David explained to his friends how he had found the gold bar. "In the carriage I saw a ba
labeled R.J."

"So what?" Josh asked, confused.

"R.J., doesn't that mean anything to you?"

"Rachel Jones!" Lily cried.

"We have to find the gold bar; it's our only evidence against Platte," Josh said,
looking around.

"Oh, no! He's disappeared again. Can you see him?" Lily asked her friends.

The crowd of actors and horses hid Platte from the detectives' view. They had
just decided to leave their post and start looking for the thief again when Frank and Tony
arrived with the search warrant. David quickly filled them in on what had happened, and
they decided to separate into two groups to search for the thief—it'd be easier to find
him that way.

Lily, David, and Josh had so much trouble finding Platte in the crowd that they
finally sent Robinson to locate him. The cockatoo didn't need to be asked twice, and flew
off to survey the crowd. After a few minutes, he signaled to the detectives that he had
found Platte by flying in little circles in the air and squawking loudly.

"Do you guys see him?" David asked.

"There!" Josh pointed.

 **QUESTION:** Where is Platte?

CLUE TWELVE: Dead End

The three friends quickly found Tony and Frank searching around the wagons and the entire group hurried to join Robinson. Robinson was perched on a rooftop just above where Platte was sitting on a horse's back, the bag marked R.J. attached to his saddle. The detectives snuck up on the thief as quietly as possible, but Platte saw them and galloped away.

They sprinted after him, but the thief was on horseback and could move much faster than they could. Audience members were starting to trickle in to see the show. They started to wonder if this chase scene was part of the show, which wasn't supposed to start for another hour. Luckily for the detectives, the crowd of people was growing denser by the minute and it kept Platte from moving as quickly as before. Josh, David, and Lily caught up to the thief after politely elbowing a few people out of the way. When they finally cornered Platte, they found him very calm and sure of himself. The bag was no longer hanging from his saddle.

"You again!" he said rudely. "Are you looking for something?"

The detectives had to face the facts: Platte had ditched the bag somewhere.

"Where could he have hidden it?" Lily lamented.

"Maybe he has an accomplice," Tony suggested.

"Maybe he does," panted Frank, who had finally caught up to the detectives. "Maybe I can tell you where he is."

 **QUESTION:** Where is Platte's accomplice?

CLUE THIRTEEN: Platte's Accomplice

Frank spotted Platte's accomplice heading toward the cliffs surrounding the quarry. The bag was attached to his belt. This stranger took advantage of the time the detectives spent arguing with Platte to sneak off with the gold bar.

The detectives left Platte and ran after the stranger, but he had a big head start. David, who was the fastest of the three, nearly caught up with him but tripped on a root jutting out of the ground. When the others caught up, the accomplice was out of sight.

"Are you okay?" Lily asked, helping David to his feet.

"Yeah," groaned David. "He can't be far away."

The group got as far as the next crossroads. "Did you see which way he went?" Lily asked, out of breath.

"No," David replied. "But I did notice that he only had three fingers on his left hand."

"That doesn't help us very much," Josh sighed.

"Not right now," David agreed.

The group decided to separate again, but Tony suddenly announced that it wasn' worth it. "I know where he went. Follow me!"

 **QUESTION:** How did Tony know which way to go?

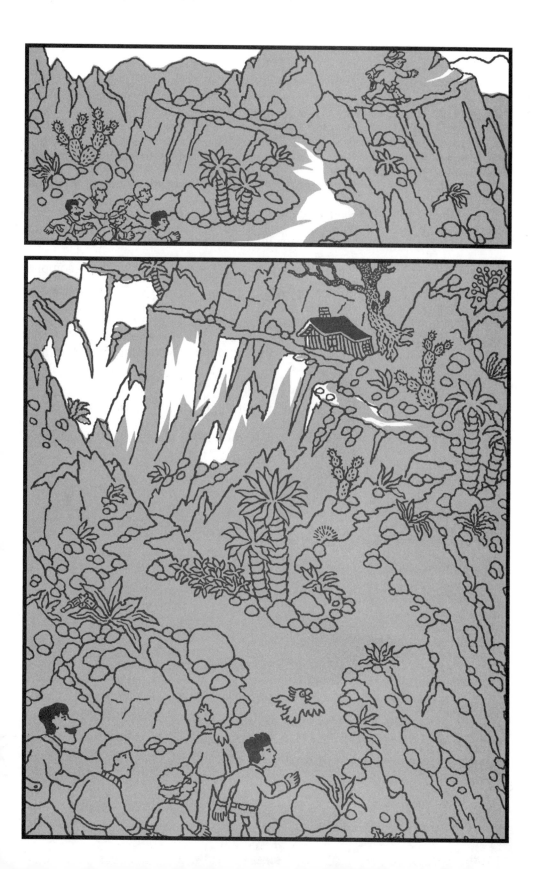

CLUE FOURTEEN: Cul-de-Sac

During his escape, Platte's accomplice had accidentally dropped the gun that was part of his costume. Tony discovered it next to a plant on the side of one of the paths.

The path stretched between two cliffs, and was so narrow that the detectives had to walk single file. After a few minutes, they hit a dead end. The path stopped abruptly, intersected by a rockslide. The detectives searched all over for a place the accomplice could have escaped through, but found nothing.

"He couldn't have just vanished!" said Frank, astonished.

David sent Robinson to fly over the rocks and investigate, but he couldn't find anything, either.

Tony was just about to propose that the group retrace their steps when they heard Lily call out from behind a nearby rock. "Over here!"

"Did you find him?" the others asked, baffled.

"No, I think he's long gone, but I know he changed his clothes before he left."

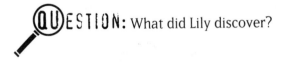 **QUESTION:** What did Lily discover?

CLUE FIFTEEN: Looking for Cinderella

Lily had found one of the accomplice's shoes.

"I don't think he could escape barefoot," she said. "He must have changed out o his costume so he could run away faster."

After a quick investigation of the scene, Lily found the rest of the accomplice's clothes, which were rolled in a ball and stuffed under a big rock.

"He must have been the one to start the rockslide to block our path," Frank concluded.

"And then he went back to join the crowd!" Josh added. The detectives turned around and headed back toward the quarry, where the show was about to start.

"How are we going to find him in there? We don't even know what he's wearing Lily asked, defeated.

"That's true, Lily, but don't forget that he has one very distinguishing characteristic," David reminded her.

The group hurried back to the quarry. The detectives looked carefully, but they couldn't find Platte's three-fingered accomplice.

"Maybe I was wrong, and he didn't come back to the village," Josh said sheepishly.

"No!" Frank reassured him. "You were right. He's here."

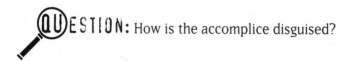 **QUESTION:** How is the accomplice disguised?

CLUE SIXTEEN: The Bearded Lady

"Talk about a costume!" Josh exclaimed. "He might have had the time to change his clothes, but not to shave!"

Platte's accomplice was dressed as a woman and holding a basket with the gold bar in it! As soon as he realized that he had been sighted, the three-fingered man sprinted off. Once again, the detectives chased after him. The man had already run a lon way, and the long hem of his dress was slowing him down. The accomplice ran through the doors of the saloon to hide, but the detectives were hot on his trail.

The saloon was bustling; the show had begun. The detectives looked around the crowded room, but the man with three fingers was nowhere to be found.

"This guy is like the invisible man!" Lily exclaimed. "*Now* where has he gone?"

David and Josh waited outside for any sign of the accomplice while Frank, Tony, and Lily searched every corner of the saloon. It was Tony who finally found him.

 QUESTION: How did Tony find the three-fingered man?

CLUE SEVENTEEN: The Show's Over

The edge of the three-fingered man's dress was sticking out from under the door of the closet he was hiding in. He must have shut the door in a hurry.

"Come out, you're surrounded!" Tony ordered, taking his gun out from his holster

The closet door creaked open and the man came out with his hands up. Everyone in the saloon suddenly grew quiet. They all thought this was part of the show!

The man with three fingers allowed himself to be handcuffed, protesting his innocence the whole time. Tony rummaged through the closet, but couldn't find the bag with the gold bar in it anywhere.

Eventually, the *real* show started up again in the saloon.

Tony brought the three-fingered man to the police station while the others stayed behind to search for the gold bar. Lily eventually found it in a funny hiding place and the detectives wrapped up another successful mystery.

 QUESTION: Where was the gold bar hidden?

CLUE ONE: Living Death

The three-fingered man hid the bag under the piano cover before hiding himself in the closet. The gold bar was inside the bag, proving the guilt of both Thomas Platte and his accomplice.

A few uneventful weeks later, David, Lily, and Josh were at the Sugar Shack talking about how much they wished they had another mystery to solve.

Robinson interrupted the conversation by flying in through a window and dropping a newspaper at their feet. "You stole Frank's paper again!" David chided his pet cockatoo gently. Robinson nibbled on David's fingers affectionately.

"Look!" said Lily, opening the newspaper. "There's an article in here about Oscar Pick!"

"Who's that?" Josh asked.

"A man who's famous for cheating in the casinos," David explained.

"But no one can ever prove he's guilty," Lily added.

"So what happened? Did they arrest him?" Josh asked.

"No," Lily replied, skimming the article. "He died."

"Let me see!" The boys replied in unison. Lily passed the newspaper to Josh.

"Wonder how he did it," David mused to himself. "Another secret carried to the grave."

"Yeah, assuming he's actually dead!" Josh replied.

QUESTION: Why does Josh doubt that Oscar Pick is dead?

CLUE TWO: The Burial

Josh explained to his friends, "The newspaper is dated June fifth; the picture of the casino was taken on the fourth; and Pick supposedly died on the second."

"Yeah, so what?" asked Lily, who was getting impatient.

"So if he really died on the second, what is he doing standing next to the casino on the fourth?!"

David looked at the newspaper. Pick was certainly in the photo, standing just to the right of the casino.

"Should we check it out for ourselves?" Lily proposed.

Two days later, the friends met up at the cemetery to find out whether Pick was actually being buried. They walked over to Pick's burial site and discovered that the grave had already been dug. The detectives were a little early for the funeral, so they decided to take a walk around the cemetery and come back later for the ceremony.

A few minutes before the funeral was supposed to begin, the detectives hid behind a nearby fence so they could see what was going on but couldn't be seen by anyone else. The funeral procession trickled in. Only a few people had come to the cemetery for Pick's funeral.

"Do you think Pick is actually inside the coffin?" Lily asked.

"The men carrying it seem to be struggling, so we know it's not empty," Josh said.

"I think I know why it's so heavy," David announced.

 QUESTION: What's in the coffin?

CLUE THREE: Ghost Story

While the detectives had explored the cemetery before the funeral, David had noticed a big pile of bricks on the grass next to the church. The bricks were no longer there once the burial began. Someone must have put the bricks in the coffin so everyone would believe that Oscar Pick's corpse was inside!

"You've got to have a really good reason to want to convince people that you're dead," Josh commented to his friends.

"Yeah, but what is it?" Lily asked.

David shook his head. He didn't know why either. This whole story seemed really crazy to him.

After the burial ended, the detectives waited until the coast was clear before leaving their hiding place behind the fence. They decided to alert Frank and Tony about their weird story.

"This is crazy!" David cried. "A dead person who isn't actually de—"

"Shh!" Lily cut him off. "Not so loud! Someone's spying on us."

QUESTION: How does Lily know that someone is watching them?

CLUE FOUR: False Alarm

Lily discreetly pointed to one of the windows of the cemetery's old storage building. David and Josh caught a glimpse of a man's face looking down at them before he disappeared behind the curtains. The detectives walked around the storage building, hoping to catch the man who was watching them or to pick up clues. The man must have realized that they had seen him, because he was nowhere to be found.

"This story keeps getting weirder and weirder," David said as the detectives explored the empty storage room.

Josh, David, and Lily looked around the storage room for clues, but they didn't find anything suspicious.

Suddenly Robinson squawked loudly, his sign that someone was coming. The detectives hid themselves as well as they could in one corner of the room. Robinson landed on a beam high up in the rafters.

"False alarm," Lily announced. "Robinson just found some new friends." Several baby birds squawked in their nest, crying for food.

"I don't like this place at all," said Josh, creeped out. "Can we go?"

"We haven't found anything yet," Lily reminded him.

"Yes we have!" David declared. "I think that was Pick himself spying on us just now. Look at this clue!"

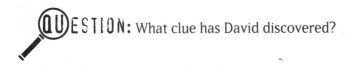

QUESTION: What clue has David discovered?

CLUE FIVE: The Queen of Spades

David picked up a piece of paper from the floor with Pick's name written on it. It looked like a coupon for a free dinner at The Queen of Spades. The detectives hurried back to the Sugar Shack with this new piece of evidence.

"The Queen of Spades . . ." Frank murmured, back at the detectives' headquarter in the Sugar Shack. "Isn't that the card room on Kings Road?"

"Yeah, and it's not one of the better ones," Tony added.

"Then it sounds like the perfect place to continue our investigation," David chimed in.

The detectives, accompanied by Frank and Tony, arrived at The Queen of Spades at nightfall.

"You guys stay out here," Tony warned the kids. "It's forbidden for minors to go inside."

"You can watch through the window," Frank added. "But be discreet!"

Lily, David, and Josh stationed themselves outside one of the windows while Frank and Tony entered the club. There were a lot of people crowded around the tables, but it didn't seem like the glamorous club they had heard so much about.

"All the people playing cards look totally honest," David said, barely hiding his disappointment.

"Not all of them," Josh corrected him. "I can assure you that some of them are cheating."

 QUESTION: Where is the cheater that Josh found?

CLUE SIX: The Secret Boot

Josh was clearly talking about the woman who had hidden the ace of hearts in her left boot. Josh knocked on the window and, once he got their attention, motioned to Tony and Frank to come outside. Josh told them what he saw. Tony and Frank went back to the bar and acted like everything was normal.

As time passed, the three friends became bored. They waited for almost an hour before the cheater stood up, asked for her winnings, and left the bar quickly. Tony and Frank paid their tab and followed her outside. The three detectives trailed behind, making sure they left enough space between themselves and the cheater so that she wouldn't notice them.

"I have a feeling I've seen her before," said Lily.

"Of course!" cried Josh, who had the same feeling. "She was at the burial earlier!"

"She doesn't seem to be too upset about it," Frank observed.

"She must be in on the plan," David concluded.

The group soon arrived at a big intersection, but the woman had disappeared. Frank and the three kids ran ahead, hoping to catch up with her.

"You'll never catch her like that," Tony said. "She's too far ahead."

 **QUESTION:** How did Tony find the woman?

CLUE SEVEN: Dead End

"Follow me! I know a shortcut." Tony sprinted down a little street without taking the time to explain to the others that he had seen the woman jump into a pickup truck after putting her boots in the back. The group ran ahead, hoping to cut the truck off before it passed them. Unfortunately, the truck passed right under their noses, and sped away before they could react.

"Too late! There's no way to know where she's going," Lily said with a sigh.

"There is a way, but we can't do anything about it tonight," said Tony. He promised to use the truck's license plate number to look up its owner's address.

"With any luck, we'll find it," he told the detectives. They planned to meet the next morning.

Thanks to a police file, Tony succeeded in finding the address, which was located a little way outside of town. The following morning, the detectives found themselves in front of a windmill, in the middle of the countryside.

"No truck, no boots, no woman. This looks like a dead end. Are you sure this is the right address?" Josh asked.

"Oh, yes, I'm completely sure," Frank answered.

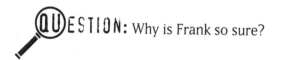 QUESTION: Why is Frank so sure?

CLUE EIGHT: Topsy-Turvy

Tony recognized the truck's license plate, which was now attached to a tractor.

"She not only cheats at cards, she also traffics illegal license plates," David commented as the group approached the mill. Before entering, the detectives peeked through all the windows to make sure that no one was inside.

"It seems that our cheater has disappeared," Lily said. "Let's hope that she left us a clue so we know where to find her."

"Let's hope," Tony replied, signaling for the rest of the group to hurry up and get inside.

The detectives searched the mill from top to bottom. While Tony dug through giant sacks of grain, Frank searched for any objects that might belong to the woman, and David, Lily, and Josh carefully replaced anything that they might have disturbed in their search of the mill. Still nothing.

Josh proposed that they climb up a ladder to the very top of the mill to take a look around. At the top, David was the one to discover the first interesting clue.

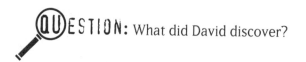 QUESTION: What did David discover?

CLUE NINE: The False Card

David noticed a playing card propped up on a beam—the jack of clubs. He grabbed the card and hurried back down the ladder to show Frank and Tony. The brothers had something interesting to show David, too. They had found an old rucksack with a comb, an empty soda can, and a full deck of cards inside. The design on the card exactly matched the one David held in his hand.

"The deck isn't missing the jack of clubs by any chance, is it?" David asked hopefully.

"I don't think so," Frank replied. "I counted the cards and there are exactly fifty-two."

David was surprised. It seemed suspicious that there were two identical cards with the jack of clubs.

"Yours must belong to another deck," Lily told David. "Unless . . ."

She took the two matching cards and placed them facedown on the table. The backs of the two cards seemed identical, all right. Lily turned the cards over and examined their faces.

"These cards are alike, but they're not exactly the same. One of them is a fake!"

QUESTION: What is the difference between the two cards?

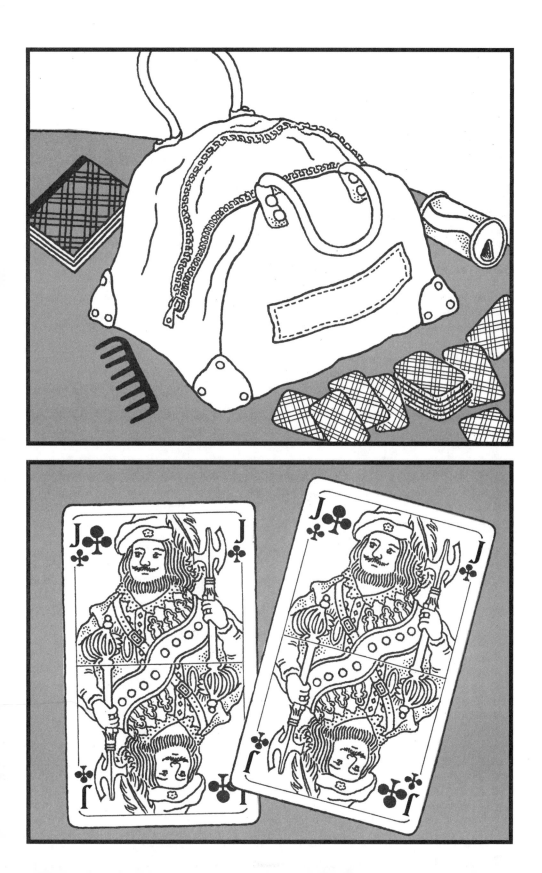

CLUE TEN: Minus One

After looking closely at the two cards, Lily noticed that on one card, the jack was wearing his ring on his middle finger, and on the other card, his ring was on his ring finger.

"Good job, Lily, but I think it's too late!" Josh hurried toward the ladder. "Someone's coming!"

The detectives heard the sound of a motor coming closer and closer to the mill. Quickly, they climbed up the ladder.

Seconds later, the detectives heard voices.

"Bingo!" David whispered to the others. "It's the living dead and his lady friend!"

Frank gestured for David to be quiet. Tony's hand was poised over his handcuffs. He could have arrested the pair of cheaters on the spot, but he preferred to wait and see what they were up to.

For a few moments the mill was strangely silent. Suddenly, a loud noise made them all jump.

"What was that?" they heard a voice cry out. Yup, it was Oscar Pick, all right.

Josh, David, Lily, Tony, and Frank didn't dare make a sound.

"It's nothing, darling. It must have been Winky," a woman's voice replied.

"Winky? It that another accomplice?" Lily asked in a whisper.

"Not exactly," answered Josh, smiling.

 **QUESTION:** Who is Winky?

CLUE ELEVEN: Brainteaser

Winky was the name of the owl that had just flown into the mill through a broke window and was now eyeing Robinson. She approached the cockatoo slowly and nuzzle against him. Robinson fluffed up his chest to look as handsome as possible.

"Robinson, this really isn't the time," David groaned. He was afraid that the bird flirtation would somehow reveal their hiding place.

Fortunately, the criminals were too busy to pay attention to what was going on above their heads in the mill's rafters. Oscar Pick took two pieces of paper out of his pocket and handed them to his accomplice.

"Tomorrow at four! Do you know where to go? Good, then you don't have to kee this with you. We wouldn't want to carry around any incriminating evidence."

Pick put the two pieces of paper on the table and left the mill. His accomplice followed closely behind.

Once they were sure the coast was clear, the detectives climbed back down the ladder and rushed over to see what Pick's two pieces of paper said. The smaller of the two scraps of paper had four dots and an X on it. The other piece of paper had a hand-drawn map on it. There were no words on either piece of paper.

"What a brainteaser," Frank said happily. "Give me the papers and I'll figure out where they're meeting!"

QUESTION: Where is the meeting?

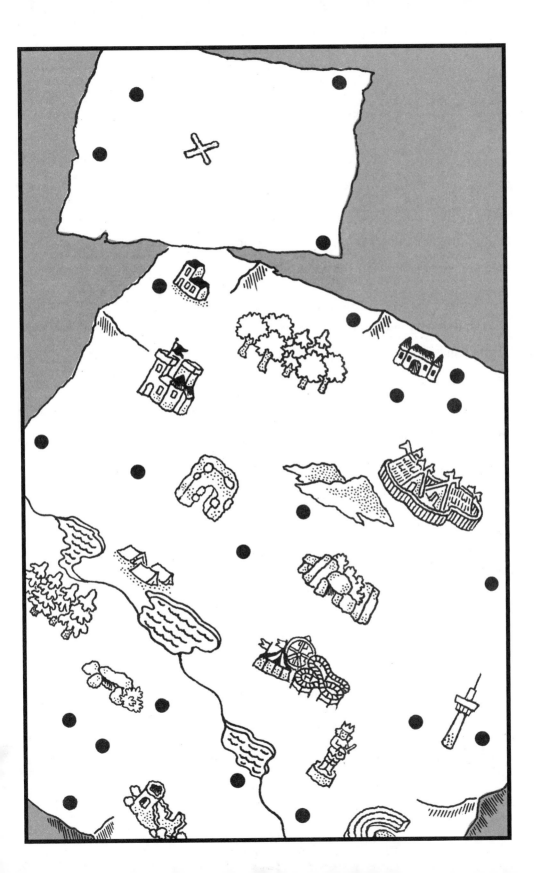

CLUE TWELVE: Double or Nothing

Frank spent the night puzzling over the two maps, and finally figured out where the crooks were meeting. In order to solve the puzzle, he superimposed the two sheets of paper, trying to find a way to make the dots overlap. The X marked a spot between the quarry and the radio tower, just above the amusement park. Frank looked at maps of the area to figure out the name of their meeting place. It was an old mine that had been turned into the Temple of Illusion, a thrill ride.

The detectives couldn't wait to investigate the Temple of Illusion. It was an exciting and mysterious place, where projectors made strange, blurred pictures appear on the columns and walls of the mine. Thrill seekers walked through the creepy mine for a fun and scary adventure. In the mine, the detectives were having such a good time that they had almost forgotten why they were there when they heard the distinct sound of footsteps running away.

"Come out, Pick! I know you're there!" Tony ordered after he saw the man's shadow on the wall.

Pick was cornered; there was only one way out of the mine. He decided to turn himself in.

"And your accomplice?" Tony asked Pick as he put the cuffs on his wrists.

Pick feigned surprise. "What accomplice?"

"That one!" David said, pointing.

 QUESTION: Where is Pick's accomplice hiding?

CLUE THIRTEEN: The Key to the Mystery

Pick's accomplice was trying to camouflage herself amongst the boulders in the background of the mine, but David saw her face. She, too, was forced to surrender. Before allowing Tony to put the second set of cuffs on her, she attempted to ditch the two little bags she was holding, but Lily saw what she was doing and recovered the bags. Each bag contained a huge sum of money.

Once they had the two criminals handcuffed, it seemed like the case was closed. But suddenly Pick made a quick motion with his hands. At first, it looked like he was trying to shake his fist at Tony and the detectives, because he was angry they had caught him. In reality, Pick was trying to get rid of something, something so small that the detectives couldn't even see what it was. The tiny object hit the ground with a metallic clang.

"Looks like we're going to have to find a needle in a haystack," Tony announced. "Because I doubt very much that our friend Pick here is going to tell us what he just threw away."

David and Lily were prepared to search the entire mine for the object, but Josh stopped them. "Don't worry guys, I've got it!"

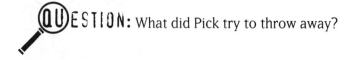

QUESTION: What did Pick try to throw away?

CLUE FOURTEEN: The Trump Card

Josh held a small key in his hand. He had found it between two rocks by following the sound it had made when it hit the ground.

Pick seemed furious, but he still tried to play dumb. Tony turned to Pick's accomplice and held up the two bags for her to see.

"I suppose this is the money you won at The Queen of Spades?"

"No, um, that's my retirement savings," the woman lied.

"She lies, she cheats—she's perfect for you, Pick!" Tony said dryly. Pick didn't respond.

"We have to find out what this key opens," Tony said.

"It's too small for a door," Josh remarked.

"And too big for an ordinary padlock," David added.

"In any case, it certainly opens something in this mine, or Pick wouldn't have bothered to hide it from us," Frank concluded.

"Yeah, but what?" Tony asked, thinking about the endless possible hiding places in the dark and shadowy mine.

"Easy," Lily said, much to everyone's surprise. "They marked the place with a series of distinct signs."

Pick and his girlfriend fumed: Their secret was out.

QUESTION: What signals did the crooks use, and how did Lily figure them out?

CLUE FIFTEEN: Bonus Round

Lily realized that all four suits in a deck of cards—clubs, hearts, spades, and diamonds—appeared on the two columns of the mine. She guessed that they had nothin to do with the projected images in the mine, and were in fact a way of pointing to a specific location. She looked in between the four signs and discovered a chest hidden among the boulders. It contained the rest of the tricksters' loot!

"Years and years of hard work!" Pick lamented. "All gone!"

"It's so unfair!" his girlfriend whined.

The double-dealing duo, who were originally headed south for a lovely vacatior ended up somewhere very different: behind bars. Pick's fake death was supposed to lessen their chances of getting caught, but the couple had the bad luck of crossing path with Lily, David, and Josh.

The police dug up the coffin, which, as David predicted, was filled with bricks.

Now that the mystery was solved, the kids thought they could finally relax. But Robinson was missing! Luckily, he flew back home three days later, exhausted but happ with an owl feather clutched in his beak.